Princess Matilda

Written and Illustrated by

Eva Montanari

Bath · New York · Singapore · Hong Kong · Cologne · Delhi · Melbourne

I am a very beautiful princess.

I live in a splendid castle
and I have a stable with three
very fast black horses.

And of course
I have many admirers,
who are all hoping one day
to become princes.

I have wonderful parties,
with friends from every corner
of my kingdom.

And I have lots of servants,
who do everything I say.

Or rather,
they're supposed to.

But sometimes they don't.
And instead they give
me orders!

Can you believe that?

I'm a very kind
and generous princess,
but when that happens,
    I get very,
        very angry…

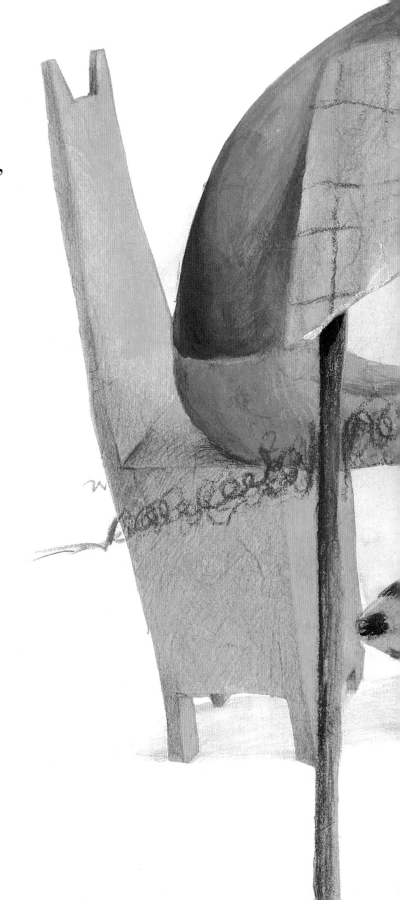

...**angry** like a witch!
I threaten to cook my
servants in a big pot
with all my frogs,
who don't want to be
princes anymore!

But can you believe that?

They're laughing!

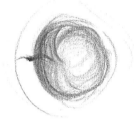

It must be because
    I'm a clown with a big red nose!

But even clowns get scolded
when they're naughty.

Well, if clowns get scolded,
then I'll be something else.

I'll be a...

...butterfly!

Flying free to the end
of the field...

...to a jungle,
where I have somewhere else to live.

There I don't need any servants.
And I don't need my princess's clothes,
or my horses, or my admirers.
I don't need my witch's hat,
or my clown's nose...

...or even my butterfly wings.

Up there I'm
a jungle woman!
I can go wherever I want.

And tonight I'm going to...

...Matilda's room.

She has a bedroom
full of dolls, bears, and toys.
And a bed that looks
just like a castle.

In she climbs,
and listens to a story
about a beautiful princess.

A princess who is also called

Matilda.

For my princesses of Strasbourg,
who lived together in a little atelier, drawing other princesses,
and sharing nice cake with a little prince inside...

This edition published by Parragon in 2010

Parragon
Queen Street House
4 Queen Street
Bath BA1 1HE, UK

Text and illustrations Copyright © 2007 Eva Montanari
The right of Eva Montanari to be identified as the author and illustrator of this work has been asserted by her in accordance with the
Copyright, Designs and Patents Act, 1988

Published by arrangement with Meadowside Children's Books, 185 Fleet Street, London EC4A 2HS.

ISBN 978-1-4454-0279-6

Printed in China